SCRUBS FOREVER!

BY
JAMIE McEWAN
ILLUSTRATIONS BY JOHN MARGESON

DARBY CREEK PUBLISHING

To Keith

Text copyright © 2008 by Jamie McEwan
Illustrations copyright © 2008 by John Margeson

Cataloging-in-Publication

McEwan, James.
Scrubs forever / by Jamie McEwan ; illustrations by John Margeson.
        p. ; cm.
ISBN 978-1-58196-069-3
Ages 8 and up.—Sequel to: Rufus the scrub does not wear a tutu.—Summary: When Dan starts to win some wrestling matches, Biff and the "in" crowd let him be part of their group. This is what Dan has always wanted, and his attitude toward the other Scrubs wavers. Will Dan realize who his real friends are?
1. Middle school students—Juvenile fiction. 2. Athletes—Juvenile fiction. 3. Rock climbing—Juvenile fiction. 4. Attitude change—Juvenile fiction. [1. Middle school students—Fiction. 2. Athletes—Fiction. 3. Rock climbing—Fiction. 4. Attitude change—Fiction.] I. Title. II. Author. III. Ill.
PZ7.M478463 Sc 2008
[Fic] dc22
OCLC: 173185964

Published by Darby Creek Publishing
7858 Industrial Parkway
Plain City, OH 43064
www.darbycreekpublishing.com

Printed in the United States of America

2 4 6 8 10 9 7 5 3 1

978 1 58196 069 3

CONTENTS

CHAPTER 1

QUOTABLE DAN

When the bell rang at the end of math class, Dan got down on the floor and started doing push-ups. Around him, students stood and picked up their books, getting ready to go to the next class.

His classmates just ignored Dan. That was because he had been doing push-ups after every class since wrestling season started. When Dan finished a set of push-ups, he'd jump up and run to his next class, where he'd do sit-ups until it started. At first the other kids had laughed and made fun of him, but after a while, they'd gotten used to it.

But this time Dan's friend Willy stopped and said, "I think you should skip the push-ups today."

"Why?" asked Dan. "'No pain, no gain!' 'No guts, no glory!'"

"Because today's the last match of the season," said Willy. "There's nothing to prepare for. You should rest up for the match."

Dan frowned. "You're right," he said, getting up and brushing off his hands. "Shoot. Last match. I've got to win it. Like the general said, 'There is no substitute for victory.'"

"Come on, you've won a bunch of matches," said Willy. "Win or lose, you've already had a good season."

"'Good is not enough when you dream of being great,'" quoted Dan.

"Dude," said Willy, "don't you get tired of all the quotations? They wear me out, I know that."

"'When the wise man speaks, the fool often sleeps,'" replied Dan.

"How many of those darned quotes do you know?" demanded Willy. "You sound like you swallowed a whole book of them."

Dan smiled to himself. He wasn't going to tell Willy, but he'd made that last one up.

CHAPTER 2

DON'T BREAK
THE HANDS

That afternoon, Dan was nervous. It was the last match of the season!

Waiting for his turn wasn't much fun. Watching his teammates wrestle just made him more nervous. His wrestling uniform seemed too tight, and his shoes seemed too loose. Dan's heart was pounding, but his hands were cold. He couldn't seem to warm them up.

"Come on, Dan, relax," said his big friend Rufus. "This is supposed to be fun, right?"

"Fun? This isn't fun. This is battle."

"It was a wrestling match, last I checked," said Rufus.

"I've just *got* to win it. You know what they say: 'Winning isn't everything. It's the *only* thing.'"

"That doesn't even make sense," said Rufus.

"Makes sense to me," said Dan.

Finally Dan's turn came. He shook hands with a tough-looking kid just his size. The whistle blew. Dan went right after him. He took his opponent down—but then the guy reversed him. Dan put the guy on his back for a second—and then the guy put Dan on his back. It went back and forth like that until Dan wasn't even sure who was on top or who was ahead.

But at the end of the match, after they shook hands, it was the other guy's hand that was raised over his head. Dan had lost.

In the locker room Dan was so mad he

kicked a locker. He raised his fists to bang on it, too, but Willy and Rufus grabbed his arms to stop him.

"I worked so hard!" yelled Dan.

"Hey, take it easy," said Rufus.

"Come on," said Willy. "So you lost a match. You're the one who's always saying, 'What doesn't kill me makes me stronger.' I don't think that's true of beating your fists on the locker, though. That just makes you injured."

"Yeah," said Rufus, "if you break your hands, you won't be able to go climbing tomorrow."

"Okay, okay," said Dan. He lay on his back on the bench. "Man, I've had it," he said. "I've really had it. I give up. I'm tired of being the smallest kid in the class. I'm tired of getting chosen last when we play volleyball at recess. I worked so hard at football! And I was still lousy. I worked so hard at wrestling! I'm telling you, I give up."

"Are you kidding me?" asked Willy. "You're the guy who's always telling us things like, 'There is no elevator to success; you have to take the stairs.'"

"And," said Rufus, "'The harder you fall, the higher you bounce!'"

"And, 'If at first you don't succeed—'"

"Can it, guys," said Dan, "I don't want to hear it."

"What I say is," said Willy, "that win or lose, the Scrubs still have fun. 'We came to play,' right?"

"No, I'm telling you, I'm tired of being a Scrub."

"Hey, man, we're proud of being Scrubs!" said Rufus.

"Not me. I tell you, I'm tired of it," said Dan.

Biff had come in from the showers while they were talking. "Yeah, you guys think you're so cool," he said, "but you're too old for that stupid Scrubs stuff. Right, Dan?" Biff was an older kid, and one of the 'in' group. He'd never been friendly with Dan.

"You think so?" asked Dan.

"Yeah," said Biff. "You've outgrown it."

CHAPTER 3
TO PULL OR NOT TO PULL

When Dan got home from school, the house was quiet. He went into his room and put on one of his CDs. He sat in his chair and looked at his posters. There were national champion wrestlers and pro-football stars and top climbers and kayakers all over his walls.

He wondered if those guys had ever lost as often as he had.

After a while, he heard his father come home. Dan found him in the kitchen getting a snack.

"Sorry I couldn't make your match today," said his father. "How'd it go?"

Dan shrugged. "Dad," he said, "you're always talking about the power of positive thinking and focus and working hard. 'Whatever you can dream, you can do.' Right?"

"That's right."

"Yeah, but—I've been really trying hard.

I really have. And I—I lost the match today. I've lost a bunch this season."

For a minute Dan's father just stared at him. Dan was afraid he was mad. But when his father finally said something, he didn't sound mad. He sounded tired.

"You know," said his father, "I'll tell you a secret. I don't succeed all the time, either. But what are we going to do? Give up?"

"The guys say I try too hard," said Dan. "That I should just have a good time."

"I want you to have a good time," said his father. "But can you try hard and still have a good time?"

Dan thought for a moment. "I'm not sure I could have a good time if I *didn't* try hard," he said.

His father laughed. "There's your answer. I'm that way, too, you know."

"So I should go ahead and do pull-ups every night like Mr. Kwan suggested?"

"He's the climbing instructor?" his father asked. Dan nodded. "You be careful out there rock climbing, okay?"

"Don't worry, Dad. It's totally safe. But how about those pull-ups? Should I?"

"Sure. Hey, I'll join you. I think I need to do some of those."

CHAPTER 4
AVOIDING EASY

Dan climbed up a cliff of overhanging gray rock. Mr. Kwan and Dan's friends watched from below. Ten feet . . . twenty feet . . . Dan was climbing fast. He was near the top when he suddenly slowed down.

"You can go to your right now," Mr.

Kwan called up to him. "It's not as steep there. It's a lot easier."

"Too easy!" Dan called back and climbed straight up the steep part.

He was thirty feet up now. The wind blew through his hair. A bird flew by below him. He was almost at the top. Dan stretched up and tried to grab a big knob of rock above him, but he couldn't quite reach it. His foot started to slip. He jammed it back into place again.

"You can do it!" called Rufus from below.

"Go, go, go!" shouted Clara.

"Go, you Scrub!" shouted Willy.

All of a sudden, Dan fell. "Agh!" he cried as he dropped off the rock and into the empty space below.

Rufus gasped. Willy started to yell something, then cut it short. Mr. Kwan moved his right hand behind him. In that right hand Mr. Kwan held a bright purple rope that went through a metal belay device. The rope ran from Mr. Kwan up to the top of the cliff through a link they called a carabiner and back down to where it was clipped to a harness around Dan's waist. Dan couldn't fall very far, because he was attached to the rope that Mr. Kwan was holding. With the belay device set, the rope couldn't slip. It stretched for a few feet and then held. Dan was brought to a gentle stop, still twenty-five feet off the ground. He hung there beside the cliff, catching his breath.

"Can I try that part again?" shouted Dan.

"No, we're running low on time," Mr. Kwan called back. "We have to give Rufus a turn."

"Just once?"

"Sorry, Dan. I'm going to lower you down."

CHAPTER 5

DAN GUESSES

When Dan was at the bottom of the cliff beside the others, he unclipped himself from the rope. Rufus clipped in and started to climb, very slowly, up the rock.

"Have you ever climbed that part where I was?" Dan asked Mr. Kwan.

"Put your right foot in that crack," Mr.

Kwan said to Rufus. "Sideways!" Then to Dan: "Yes, I have."

"Yeah, but you're tall," said Dan. "You could have reached that last hold easy."

"Well, sure, sometimes being tall helps," said Mr. Kwan. "But a lot of top climbers aren't very tall. Somebody told me that girl, Elisabeth whatever-her-name-is, climbed that route. She's not tall."

"Who's that?"

"A girl who moved here from Colorado. I saw a TV special about her."

"She's been on TV?" asked Clara.

"Yeah."

"I want to be on TV," said Dan.

"You're too ugly," said Willy. "You'd break the camera."

Dan just rolled his eyes.

Mr. Kwan frowned, but he didn't take his eyes off Rufus, who was halfway up. "Listen, Willy," said Mr. Kwan, "no insulting allowed, not even in kidding. That reminds me. You shouldn't call Dan a 'scrub,' either."

"No, no, that's not an insult," said Willy. "Rufus and Dan and I were so bad at football last year, other guys called us 'scrubs.' We decided we liked it. We're the Scrubs.

Clara's an official Scrub, too. Right Clara?"

"You bet," said Clara. "And proud of it."

"Is that right, Dan?" asked Mr. Kwan.

"Yeah, true story," said Dan. "But . . . ."

"But what?" asked Mr. Kwan. "You don't like being called a 'scrub'?"

"I guess it's all right."

"What do you mean, 'you guess'?" asked Willy.

"I mean, *I guess.*"

CHAPTER 6

LOUD LUNCH

As usual, the lunchroom was crowded. Rufus and Dan were holding their trays, trying to edge over to where Willy was sitting.

"Hey, guys, . . . wait up," said a voice behind them.

It was Clara, standing with a girl named

Lisa—a new girl in school that year. They looked funny standing together. Clara was tall and wore her blond hair in pigtails, while Lisa was the smallest kid in the class and had dark, curly hair.

"Hey, Clara," said Biff, coming out of the lunch line to stand beside them. "Does she really play basketball? I mean, she's not much bigger than the ball." Biff's friends behind him laughed.

Lisa frowned, but she didn't say anything.

"You're no giant yourself, Biff," said Clara, looking down at him. Clara was almost a half-foot taller than Biff.

"Maybe she's the team mascot," said Dan. "Little Lisa, the mascot."

"Don't you start talking trash about Lisa!" said Clara angrily.

"It doesn't matter," murmured Lisa.

"Dude," Clara said to Dan, "she's one of the Scrubs, too, you know."

"Since when is she one of the Scrubs?" asked Dan.

"Since I say she is," replied Clara. "Come on, it's not some exclusive club. She tries hard, just like you."

"Yeah," said Lisa.

"Yeah, but she's the way the Scrubs used

to be," said Biff. "Dan won over half his matches this year."

Dan looked at Biff in surprise. He wouldn't have thought Biff was keeping track.

"Okay, great, but so what?" asked Clara. "I was high scorer on our basketball team. Who cares? I'm still a Scrub at heart. And so is Lisa."

"Come on, Dan," said Biff. "Sit with us. That table's going to be too crowded anyway."

Dan hesitated. But he decided he just couldn't turn Biff down.

"I'll see you around, guys," Dan said to Rufus and Clara.

So he had lunch with Biff and his loud friends. Clara glared at him from their nearby table. Rufus and Willy looked puzzled. Lisa just kept looking down at her lunch tray.

CHAPTER 7

COOL OR CREEP

The next day was the day the Scrubs went kayaking together. Now that winter sports were over, they were alternating climbing with kayaking.

When Dan got into the van, Clara said right away, "I'm mad at you, Dan."

"Huh?" said Dan. "What did *I* do?"

"You made fun of Lisa for being small, of all things. You know how idiotic that is, coming from you? It was also mean."

"It was just a joke."

"And then you wouldn't sit with us," said Clara.

"The table was crowded," said Dan. He turned to Rufus and Willy. "Come on, guys. Was I being mean?"

Rufus shrugged.

Willy said, "Well, yeah. Kind of."

Dan stared out the window and watched the trees go by for a minute. "Okay," he said finally. "If I was mean,

I'm sorry. Tell her I'm sorry."

"Since when do you hang out with Biff, anyway?" asked Willy.

"Hey, we wrestled on the same team all season," said Dan.

"Yeah, but it's Biff! The original jerk!"

"He's changed," said Dan. "Ever since I started beating him in practice every once in a while. And winning some of my matches."

"Is that what you want?" asked Willy. "Friends who only like you when you win?"

"Maybe I want friends who are cool," said Dan. "And popular."

"Like Biff?"

"Yeah, like Biff."

"The whole reason we started the Scrubs was to stand up to creeps like Biff," said Willy.

"Yeah," said Dan. "That was fine then. But now, I'm starting to think the Scrubs thing is so . . . so grammar school."

"What do you mean?" asked Willy.

"I mean, Rufus is getting good at football and—we're getting better at wrestling and kayaking and—we're just not 'scrubs' anymore!"

"I was always good at basketball and soccer," said Clara, "but I was still a Scrub.

Being a Scrub is a state of mind. It means we don't care what everybody else thinks. It means we go for it, no matter what—like you did yesterday, going for the hard part of that cliff. It means we're not afraid to go out for ballet, like Rufus did last fall."

"Yeah, okay," said Dan. "That was fine. Now I think it's time to make some new friends."

"Be careful you don't lose the old ones along the way," said Clara.

Just then they pulled up beside the river. Everyone got out before Dan could think of anything to say.

CHAPTER 8

MYSTERY GIRL

It was raining the next time climbing practice was scheduled, so Mr. Kwan took them to the climbing gym. People were climbing up the walls all around them. Some were in the "cave," where the walls curved up into a low ceiling and thick pads covered the floor. There were holds bolted in the ceiling, and climbers clung from them, hanging upside down like spiders.

Mr. Kwan took them to a place where the wall was built out at the bottom so the climb was at an easy slant.

"Come on, can't we do something steeper?" asked Dan.

"No, this is the best place for us."

"Best place for Rufus, maybe," said Dan.

"None of that," warned Mr. Kwan.

Rufus was having the hardest time with rock climbing. Dan glanced over at him. But Rufus pretended he hadn't heard.

"Gee whiz," said Dan. "This is too easy."

"I'll tell you what," said Mr. Kwan. "When your turn comes, I'll time you. See how fast you can do it. They have competitions like that, you know. Speed climbing, they call it."

"That's cool," said Dan. "I'd like to do one of those."

"There's one coming up. You could try it, if you want."

"Sign me up!" said Dan.

"Aw, man," said Rufus, "that was what I liked about climbing—no competition. Now you're turning it into a race."

"You don't have to race, Rufus," said Mr.

Kwan. "It's kind of a special thing, anyway. It's a different skill. I'm more into getting you guys outdoors on the real stuff."

Willy was the first to climb, and Dan watched him, imagining how he would do each move.

When Dan's turn came, he pretended it was a race. He sped up the first half, but then he was panting so hard he had to rest for a moment.

"Smooth is fast! Remember to flow!" called Mr. Kwan from below. "Keep your weight in your feet," he added.

Dan started up again, trying to be

smooth, trying to keep his weight in his feet.
It seemed to help. Soon he was at the top.

After he had lowered Dan to the floor
again, Mr. Kwan said, "Good job, Dan.
That was fast."

"Do you think I could win the competition?" asked Dan.

"Yeah, you might win your age group.
Depends on who enters. Maybe that
Elisabeth kid will enter. She'd give you a
run for your money."

"Who is this mystery girl, anyway?"
asked Clara.

"You should know her," said Mr. Kwan.

"She goes to your school. I even think she's in your grade. Elisabeth—I can't remember her last name, but I think she goes by Lisa."

"A short girl? Dark, curly hair?"

"Yeah, that's right."

"You're kidding!" said Dan.

"No, that sounds like her."

"Little Lisa is the TV star from Colorado?" said Dan. "I don't believe it."

But it was true. Lisa had been on TV. There had been articles about her in the Colorado newspapers and in climbing magazines.

"Why didn't you tell us you were

famous?" Clara asked Lisa in the hall before class the next day. The four friends clustered around her.

"I'm not famous," said Lisa.

"You should come climbing with us!" said Rufus.

"Well, it's not like she's a beginner," said Clara.

"Do you ever climb in the climbing gym?" asked Dan.

"Not very much," said Lisa. "Mostly outside."

"But there's going to be a contest in a few weeks," said Clara. "One of those speed contests. You have to enter!"

"I've never done one of those," said Lisa. "But it sounds like fun."

The bell rang. "See you guys," said Lisa.

Still Dan could hardly believe it.

That night Dan did more pull-ups than he ever had before.

CHAPTER 9
SPEED CLIMBING

Everybody in school had heard about the climbing competition. A lot of them came to watch. They wanted to see if this tiny little Lisa could really climb better than most grown-ups.

There were two identical routes next to

each other on the climbing wall. The same holds had been screwed into the wall in the same places. Climbers were paired off and raced against each other. Then the winners raced off again until only two were left. And then the last two raced to decide the winner.

Dan won three times in a row to get into the finals. Dan was a lot faster than the kids he climbed against. Some of them were big, strong kids, but they didn't seem to know where to put their hands and feet.

Between heats, Dan got to watch Lisa climb. He had wondered what she would do, being so small, when a hold was out of her reach. She made it look easy. She just kind of jumped. Her feet came off her footholds. But she did it so lightly it didn't look like she was jumping at all. It looked like the most natural thing in the world, like she was walking.

Dan pointed this out to Mr. Kwan.

"You're right. She's good at those," said Mr. Kwan. "Dynamic moves, or 'dynos,' they call them."

"They're incredibly cool," said Dan.

"You do that, too, you know," said Mr. Kwan.

"I do?"

"Yeah. You do it without realizing it." Mr. Kwan looked over at him. "Don't worry, Dan. You're a good climber. You both are. Just keep it smooth. And don't forget to have fun."

When the final round came, Dan and Lisa clipped into their ropes right across from each other. Dan looked over at her and nodded.

"Good luck," said Lisa very softly.

"Yeah, you, too," said Dan.

Dan looked up at the colored holds bolted onto the wall. They had changed the holds for the finals. He didn't try to think about where he would put his hands and feet. That was too hard. He just tried to feel it. There was one spot that was particularly tricky, where he would have to jam his hands and feet between two boards. He rubbed chalk on his hands to keep the sweat from ruining his grip.

When the whistle blew, Dan started up slowly. He could see that Lisa was ahead of him. But that was all right. The hard part was still to come.

When he reached the boards, Dan really tried to speed up. He jammed his fists in, he wedged his feet, and up he went. He was panting hard by the time he got above them, and his hands felt damp and greasy on the last couple of holds. But he didn't dare take the time to chalk them again.

"Bang!" he slapped his hand on the plate at the top. He looked over.

"Bang!" went Lisa's an instant later.

Dan could feel the rope tighten up. He leaned back and relaxed. Fending off the wall with his feet, he allowed the rope to lower him to the ground.

CHAPTER 10
SHAKE, SCRUB

But Dan never reached the ground.
Before he could get his feet down, some
kids from school grabbed his legs and held
him up on their shoulders.

"Way to be!" "Dan the man!" "Yee-haw!"
they were saying.

At the back of the crowd, his father was

clapping and smiling.

It felt good to finally be number one at something, though not quite as good as he'd thought it would feel. Something was still bothering him.

Rufus, Willy, and Clara were waving at him from one side. Lisa was standing beside them, looking upset. Just then Biff came up to her.

"So, Ms. TV Star from Colorado," Biff said loudly. "You can't keep up with our guy. You're not a star any longer. You're just a loser now!"

"Let me down," Dan said to the kids

holding him. They lowered him, and Dan unclipped from the rope. He could hear Lisa saying to Clara, "This is the only thing I've ever been good at. I can't stand—"

"Boo hoo," Biff interrupted.

"Hey, Biff," said Dan, going over to them. "Leave her alone. Being mean doesn't make you cool, you know."

Dan turned to Lisa. "Don't listen to Biff," he said. "It was just a race. I barely won. Besides, you shouldn't worry about this stuff. This was just fooling around, right? You'll have to come climbing with us sometime. We'll have some fun, okay?"

"Stop being such a goody-goody, Dan," said Biff. "Let the loser cry. You're one of the guys now! You're one of us! You don't have to be nice to losers. You're not a Scrub anymore."

"Maybe I *want* to be a Scrub," said Dan. "Once a Scrub, always a Scrub."

"Yeah," said Clara. "Scrubs are allowed to win. As long as they're nice about it."

Dan turned to Lisa. "I'm sorry I was a jerk before. Shake, fellow Scrub?"

Lisa held out her hand. As they shook, she even managed to smile.

CHAPTER 11

HOLDING THE LINE

Today, Dan held the purple rope. The rope went from his right hand, through the belay device, up the cliff, through a carabiner, and back to Rufus.

And Rufus was twenty-five feet off the ground.

Only Dan held the rope. It was his job to lock it off if Rufus fell.

Dan watched Rufus's every move. As Rufus climbed, Dan pulled in the rope to take in the slack. It was important not to have too much slack.

Rufus was at a tricky spot now. The rock was mostly smooth with only a few little bumps to hold onto.

Rufus came to a stop. He started to let go of one hold to reach up for another, but then he put his hand back and clung there.

"Go, go, go!" shouted Willy.

Rufus reached up again—and started to

slip. "I'm—" he said. And then he fell.

Dan had pulled his right hand back as soon as Rufus began to slip. The rope couldn't move. Dan could feel Rufus's weight come onto the rope. If Dan hadn't been roped to a tree behind him, he would have been pulled off his feet. But the weight went into the tree, so the rope just stretched a little, and then brought Rufus to a gentle stop. It wasn't hard. Still, it was Dan's hand that kept the rope angled so the belay device remained locked.

"Okay," gasped Rufus, hanging from his harness. "Let me down to that ledge."

"Gotcha," said Dan. "I'm lowering."

Dan glanced over at Mr. Kwan. Mr. Kwan hadn't moved when Rufus fell. Now he smiled at Dan and nodded. Mr. Kwan trusted him.

Dan let the rope slip a little, then a little more, until Rufus stood on a ledge below the smooth part.

"I guess you should come down," said Mr. Kwan to Rufus. "We've still got a couple of people to go."

Dan could see Rufus slump when Mr. Kwan said that.

"Give him one more try," said Dan.

"He'll do it this time."

"Are you sure you want to take the time?" Mr. Kwan asked Dan. "You and Lisa haven't gone yet."

"If it's okay with Lisa, it's okay with me," said Dan.

"Sure thing," said Lisa. Then she called up to Rufus, "When you get to that place where you fell, put your left foot where your right foot was. That'll help your balance when you reach."

"Okay."

Again Rufus climbed while Dan carefully took in the slack. When Rufus got to the place he'd fallen, he brought his left foot up, exactly as Lisa had told him. Then he reached up with his hand and grabbed the next hold.

"Go, Rufus, you've got it!" called Clara.

Rufus continued to climb until he stood on the top of the cliff. He raised his hands over his head. "Yahoo!" he shouted, and they all cheered.

After Rufus was down again, Mr. Kwan turned to Lisa and Dan. "I'm sorry, guys," he said, "but there isn't time for both of you."

"That's okay," said Dan. "Lisa, you were going to show me how you did that overhang move, anyway. That won't take long. Let's do that."

"Are you sure she has anything to teach the 'king of speed'?" asked Clara.

"A lot," said Dan. "I may be the 'king of speed,' but Lisa's the 'queen of the over-hang.'"

Willy frowned. "While the rest of us are just Scrubs," he said.

"Come on, you know you guys are getting good," said Lisa.

"Yeah, but you're still Scrubs," said Dan. Everyone turned to stare at him. "You all are. A bunch of Scrubs." He grinned. "I know *I* am. Like I said before: 'Once a Scrub, always a Scrub.' Right, guys?"

"For sure!"

"You bet."

"Me, too!"

"Count me in," said Lisa, nodding.

"Scrubs forever," said Dan. "And proud of it."

ABOUT THE AUTHOR AND THE ILLUSTRATOR

JAMIE McEWAN grew up in Silver Spring, Maryland. He attended the Landon School for Boys, where he learned first-hand the frustrations of being a Scrub. But being a Scrub didn't last forever. Jamie went on to serve as captain of the Yale wrestling team and to win a bronze medal in the 1972 Olympics for whitewater slalom. Along the way, he developed a lifelong passion for outdoor sports.

Jamie spent many hours brushing up on his rock-climbing skills in preparation for a major whitewater expedition to the fabled Tsangpo River in Tibet. That expedition was the subject of two books and a National Geographic television special.

Scrubs Forever! is McEwan's sixth book for children and his fourth in the Scrubs series for Darby Creek Publishing. Jamie lives in upstate Connecticut with his wife, Sandra Boynton (the author, illustrator, and songwriter), their four children, and two dogs.

JOHN MARGESON has been an art director and designer for more than twenty-five years, but his true love is illustration. John resides in Westerville, Ohio. More of his work can be seen at www.johnmargeson.com.